CLASSIC
FAIRY TALES

from

HANS CHRISTIAN ANDERSEN

INTRODUCTION

Hans Christian Andersen, the Danish storyteller, was born in 1805. Although he was the son of a poor shoemaker, he longed to make his living by writing. After many struggles, he finally became known as a poet, but today it is his fairy tales that are best loved.

Perhaps the secret of Andersen's success is that he wrote his stories, as he told a friend, as if he were telling them to a child.

Each time a story is told, it changes a little, to suit its teller and its audience. Everyone has a different idea about why the characters act as they do and which part of the story is the most interesting. So these stories are not *exactly* as Hans Christian Andersen wrote them, over a hundred and fifty years ago and in a different language, but they are still full of strange and wonderful things. When you tell them to your own children, no doubt they will change a little more.

Pictures tell stories too from age to age;
Search low and high
To find a butterfly
Fluttering on every page.

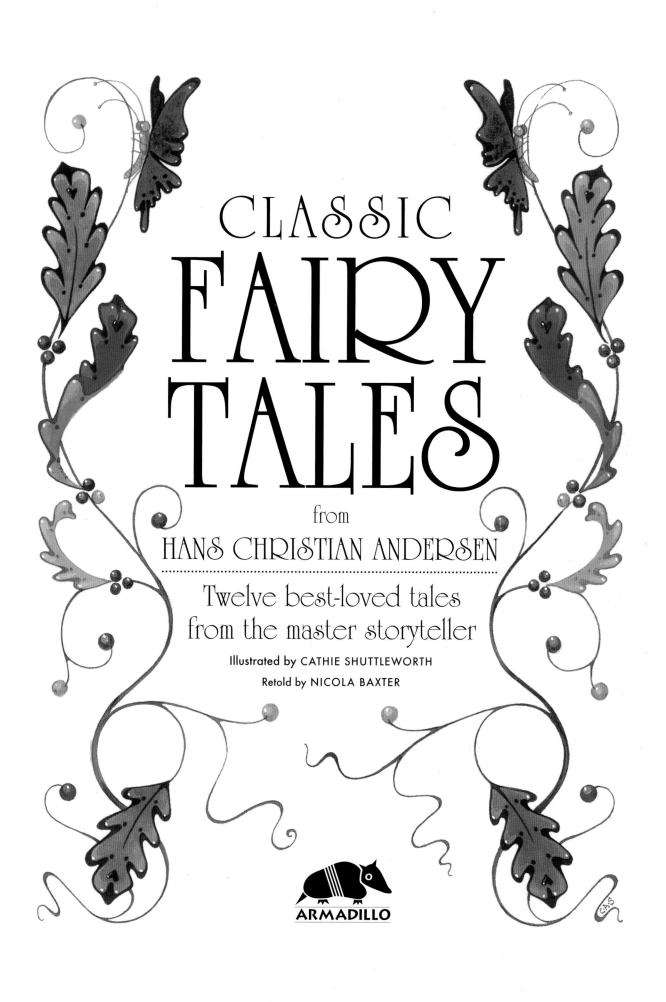

CLASSIC
FAIRY
TALES

from
HANS CHRISTIAN ANDERSEN

Twelve best-loved tales
from the master storyteller

Illustrated by CATHIE SHUTTLEWORTH

Retold by NICOLA BAXTER

ARMADILLO

FOR MY PARENTS.
C.A.S.

This edition is published by Armadillo, an imprint of Anness Publishing Ltd,
Blaby Road, Wigston, Leicestershire LE18 4SE; info@anness.com

www.annesspublishing.com

If you like the images in this book and would like to investigate using them for publishing,
promotions or advertising, please visit our website www.practicalpictures.com for more information.

Publisher: Joanna Lorenz
Produced by Nicola Baxter
Editorial consultant: Ronne Randall
Designer: Amanda Hawkes
Production controller: Don Campaniello

ETHICAL TRADING POLICY
Trees are being cultivated to replace the materials used to make this product. For further
information about our ecological investment scheme, go to www.annesspublishing.com/trees

A CIP catalogue record for this book is available from the British Library.

PUBLISHER'S NOTE
The author and publishers have made every effort to ensure that this book is safe for its intended use, and
cannot accept any legal responsibility or liability for any harm or injury arising from misuse.

Manufacturer: Anness Publishing Ltd, Blaby Road, Wigston, Leicestershire LE18 4SE, England
For Product Tracking go to: www.annesspublishing.com/tracking
Batch: 6048-20924-1127

Contents

THE LITTLE MERMAID

Once upon a time, there was a King with six beautiful daughters. However, he was not a King of the human world, but of merpeople. His lands lay far, far below the waves, where fish flash like little jewels among the reefs and craggy rocks.

The King and the six Princesses lived in a wonderful palace, made of glowing coral and gleaming shells. The girls' mother had died, but their grandmother took good care of them. Of all the Princesses, the youngest was the most beautiful. Her long hair floated around her like a golden cloud, and her tail shimmered with blue, green, and silver.

If there was one thing that the Princesses loved above all, it was to hear their grandmother tell them stories of the land above the waves. There, she told them, human beings walked on strange things called legs. And extraordinary fish swam through the air, flapping their long fins.

The more the old merwoman talked of this strange world, the more the youngest mermaid longed to see it.

"When you are fifteen," her grandmother promised, "you shall go."

When the eldest Princess was old enough, she swam to the surface, returning the next day to tell of the wonderful things she had seen.

"There are glittering cities," she said, "with twinkling lights and the sound of humans laughing. And there are huge ships, as large as palaces, that sail across the sea in the sunshine."

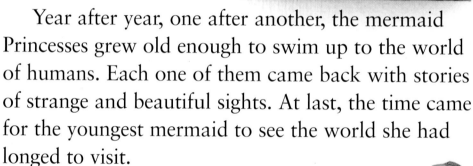

Year after year, one after another, the mermaid Princesses grew old enough to swim up to the world of humans. Each one of them came back with stories of strange and beautiful sights. At last, the time came for the youngest mermaid to see the world she had longed to visit.

As she rose to the surface for the first time, the sun was just setting, tingeing the sky with pink and gold. Nearby, a fine ship was drifting gently, for there was very little wind. As the little mermaid watched, a handsome Prince came onto the deck and looked out across the sea. He did not know that he was being watched, or that the little mermaid could not take her eyes from his face.

Darkness fell, and the ship began to toss as the wind rose. A dreadful storm wrenched away the sails and the rigging, and huge waves crashed onto the deck, tearing apart the planks. As the ship sank, the little mermaid caught sight of the Prince, struggling in the water.

Before long, the Prince closed his eyes, too tired to stay afloat any longer. But the little mermaid held up his head and guided him gently to shore. When morning came, the wind dropped and the sun rose. The little mermaid stayed near the shore, so that she could watch over the sleeping Prince.

Before long, some girls from the nearby town came down to the sea. The Prince woke as they bent over him on the sand, smiling as they helped him away. Only the little mermaid felt sad. She feared that she would never see him again.

After that, the little mermaid often rose to the surface, eager for a sight of the Prince. She watched his beautiful palace from the nearby sea and sometimes saw him walking among his courtiers. Yet she grew sadder and sadder, until she could not bear it any more. She decided to go to see the Water Witch.

The Water Witch lived in a deep, dark part of the ocean, where water snakes writhed in the cold water. When she saw the little mermaid, she laughed.

"I know why you have come," she said. "You want to go and live in the human world, so that you can be near the Prince. You want me to turn your mermaid's tail into human legs, ugly as they are. But do you know the price you will have to pay?"

"No," whispered the Princess, "but I will pay it gladly to be human."

"I shall need your voice, with which you sing so sweetly," said the witch. "Then I can turn you into a human girl, as lovely as any that walks on Earth. But remember, if the Prince does not love you with all his heart and take you for his wife, you will turn into sea foam and be lost forever. You can never return to your home beneath the waves."

"Hurry," said the mermaid. "I have already decided."

So the Water Witch gave the little mermaid a potion to drink. The Princess rose to the surface and swam beneath the Prince's palace. A terrible sadness overwhelmed her as she drank the potion, for she knew how much she was leaving behind.

But that sadness was forgotten when she stood for the first time before the Prince she loved. He at once wanted to meet the beautiful stranger and, although she could not speak to him, he soon found that he could not bear to be apart from her, but kept her always by his side.

The little mermaid loved the young man more each day, but he never thought of marrying her. "You remind me of a girl who once saved me from drowning," he said. "She is the only one I could ever really love." The poor little mermaid could not tell him that he had already met her.

Months passed, and the Prince's mother and father urged him to find a bride. At last he agreed to meet a Princess in a nearby country. Of course, the little mermaid went with him on the royal ship, although she felt as if her heart were breaking.

When the Prince stepped on shore and met the new Princess for the first time, he was so dazzled by her beauty that he believed he was meeting the girl who had saved him from the sea. "It is you!" he cried. "I have found the girl I shall love for the rest of my life."

Preparations for the wedding were made at once. It was a magnificent affair, with flowers and silks and jewels. Everyone cheered with joy to see the happy pair. Only the little mermaid was silent, and her tears fell unseen.

That night, as the Prince and his bride were guided to their cabin on the royal ship, the little mermaid stood on deck and gazed at the dark water. At dawn, she would be turned into foam, never to see, or hear, or love again.

But as she stood there, the little mermaid's sisters rose to the surface of the water. Their flowing hair was cut short.

"We gave it to the Water Witch," they said, "in return for this knife. If you kill the Prince tonight, you will be free of the spell and can return to live with us in your home under the sea."

The little mermaid took the knife, but when she stood above the sleeping Prince, she knew that she could never harm him. Weeping, she flung the knife away and plunged into the sea.

But instead of turning into foam, the little mermaid found herself floating in the air, the ship sailing on far below. Around her were lovely creatures made of golden light.

"We are the daughters of the air," they said. "By doing kind acts for others, we gain happiness ourselves. You belong with us, little mermaid, where you can be happy at last."

As the little mermaid rose into the sunshine, she looked down at the Prince and his bride, standing on the deck of the ship. And for the first time in a long, long while, she smiled.

THUMBELINA

Sometimes wishes do come true. There was once a woman who longed above everything else to have a little girl of her own. She went to a wise old woman to ask for advice.

"I want so much to have a little tiny girl to care for," she told the old woman.

"That is easy, my dear," said the old woman. Take this barley seed and plant it in a pot. It is no ordinary seed, as you will see."

So the woman went home and planted the seed. Almost at once, a green shoot appeared. It quickly grew into a strong plant, with one large bud. When the bud opened, there was a beautiful red and yellow flower, a little like a tulip.

The astonished woman bent and kissed the lovely petals, and at that very moment, the flower opened. In the middle sat a little tiny girl, perfect in every way.

Because she was no bigger than the woman's thumb, she was called Thumbelina.

There never was a little girl who was loved so much or cared for so well. She had a walnut shell for a cradle and rose leaves for a blanket, while violet flowers made a pretty pillow for her head.

As her mother worked around the house during the day, Thumbelina played on the table. She had a shallow dish of water, with a lily leaf in the middle, and she loved to row herself back and forth in the sunlight from the open window. As she rowed, she sang so sweetly that even the birds outside stopped to listen to her.

So Thumbelina was happy, until one night a mother toad hopped through the window and saw the tiny girl in her pretty bed.

"She would make a beautiful wife for my son," thought the toad, and she picked up the sleeping girl and carried her back to the riverbank.

So that Thumbelina could not escape, the toad put her on a lily leaf in the middle of the river. The little girl was not frightened, for she remembered her days playing on the table, but she did want to go home, and she did not want to marry the toad's son.

When the toad hopped away to make a house for her son in the reeds, Thumbelina sat on her leaf and sobbed. A little fish heard her crying and popped up his head.

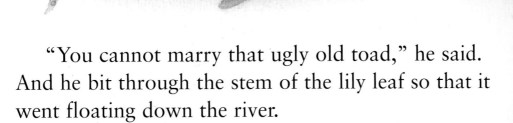

"You cannot marry that ugly old toad," he said. And he bit through the stem of the lily leaf so that it went floating down the river.

Thumbelina felt happier now. She passed many beautiful places, and a butterfly flew down to visit her.

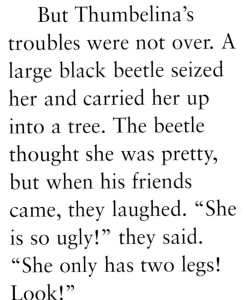

But Thumbelina's troubles were not over. A large black beetle seized her and carried her up into a tree. The beetle thought she was pretty, but when his friends came, they laughed. "She is so ugly!" they said. "She only has two legs! Look!"

The beetle carried Thumbelina down to a flowery meadow and left her there. He could not bear to hear his friends laugh at him. And so, Thumbelina passed the summer quite happily, drinking nectar from the flowers and playing with her friends the butterflies.

But gradually, the days began to grow shorter. Winter was coming, and the nights were cold. Thumbelina knew that she could not survive the winter without a home to live in. As the first flakes of snow began to fall, she wrapped herself in a dry leaf and set off to find shelter.

Just as the shivering girl began to lose hope, she met a busy little mouse. "You can stay with me, in my little house," said the mouse kindly.

Thumbelina was happy in the snug little home, until the mouse's friend came to visit. He was a mole who lived underground, and he soon fell in love with Thumbelina and wanted to marry her.

"You are lucky," said the mouse. "The mole is rich. You will never want for anything again."

One day, the mole took Thumbelina to see his underground home. As they walked along a dark passageway, the mole warned her, "Be careful here. Something has died and is lying in the way."

Thumbelina knelt down. She felt that it was a beautiful bird, and his little heart was still feebly beating.

Thumbelina took care of the bird, and by spring, it was ready to fly away to join its friends. Thumbelina watched it fly away, and wished that she too could escape. She knew that when winter came again, she would have to marry the mole and live underground for the rest of her life.

Summer passed again, and autumn leaves were rustling around her feet as Thumbelina stood and looked at the blue sky for the last time. She felt a terrible sadness pressing down on her.

Just then, a voice from above called to her. "Come with me! I'm flying to a warmer country for the winter. You will love it there." It was the bird she had rescued almost a year before!

In no time at all, Thumbelina was sitting on the bird's back, soaring over fields and cities. The bird flew over mountains, lakes, and the stormy sea. At last he came to rest in a warm, sunny country, where orange trees grew and the air was full of the scent of beautiful flowers.

The swallow set Thumbelina down on a leaf among the flowers. You can imagine how surprised she was to see a little man, no bigger than herself, sitting among the petals.

"Welcome to my country," he said. "I am the Prince of all the flower people. We are so happy to see you, we will call you Maia."

So the little girl was happy at last. She fell in love with the Prince and married him, and her lovely voice was often heard singing sweetly in the scented air.

THE EMPEROR'S NEW CLOTHES

Some Emperors like nothing better than to wage war on three nearby kingdoms before breakfast. Some love to build beautiful castles and palaces, each one bigger and better than the last. But the Emperor in this story had a more unusual passion: he loved clothes. It was well known that the Emperor spent most of the day trying on one costume after another to find which was most flattering to the (rather generous) royal figure.

One day there came to the court a pair of rascals intent on making a little money and living an easy life. They let it be known that they were weavers ~ and not just ordinary ones. "The cloth that we weave," they said, "is so extraordinarily fine, and its pattern is so rare and intricate, that only the most intelligent and refined people can see it."

Before long, news of the two so-called weavers reached the ears of the Emperor. "How very useful," he said to himself. "If I wore a suit of that cloth, I would be able to tell at once which of my ministers were too stupid and ill bred for their jobs." So he summoned the weavers before him.

When they arrived at the court, the two mischief makers bowed low. "What is Your Imperial Highness's pleasure?" they asked.

"I would like a suit made entirely of your famous cloth," declared the Emperor, "and I would like it by the end of the week!"

"No problem at all," replied the weavers reassuringly. "Now, if we could just take a few measurements. ... My, my, Your Highness has the figure of a man of ... *ahem* ... twenty!"

Next the weavers ordered bales of costly silk and gold thread, to weave, they said, into their famous cloth. They had two enormous looms set up in a comfortable room. All day long they sat in front of the looms, pretending to weave. Of course, the looms were completely empty.

The Emperor was anxious to see how his suit was coming along, but although he knew that he was the cleverest man in the land, he was just a little worried that he might not be able to see the cloth.

The Emperor thought long and hard (in fact, surprisingly long and hard for the cleverest man in the land) until he had an idea.

"Summon my Chief Minister!" he cried. "He can report to me on the cloth the weavers are making for me."

Well, the Chief Minister couldn't see the cloth either. But he was very worried that the Emperor might dismiss him if he was one of those unfortunate people who were too stupid to see it. "It's absolutely perfect for Your Highness," he reported. "I can honestly say that I have never seen anything to match it."

Every day, the weavers called for more silk and gold. They packed this away in their luggage, ready for a quick getaway!

Soon the Emperor became impatient again. He sent his Chancellor to inspect the work. Once again, the poor man could see nothing at all, but he did not want to lose his job. "It is beyond compare," he declared. "Your Highness will be really delighted."

At last the Emperor could bear it no longer. He hurried along to the room where the weavers were working and flung open the doors.

The weavers, who had heard the swish of royal robes in the corridor, were very busy at their looms. Their hands darted backward and forward, holding ... absolutely nothing!

The Emperor stopped dead. It was his worst nightmare! Only he, of all his court, was too stupid to see the wonderful cloth. His throat felt dry and his voice quavered as he announced, "The Chief Minister and the Chancellor were too faint in their praise. This cloth is truly too beautiful for words!"

At the end of the week there was to be a Grand Procession. Naturally, it was expected that the Emperor would wear clothes of the famous new cloth, of which the whole empire had heard. The weavers were busy night and day, cutting thin air with huge pairs of scissors, sewing with invisible thread, and pretending to sew on buttons and braid. When they were tired of this, they smiled at each other and said, "There! A costume fit for an Emperor!"

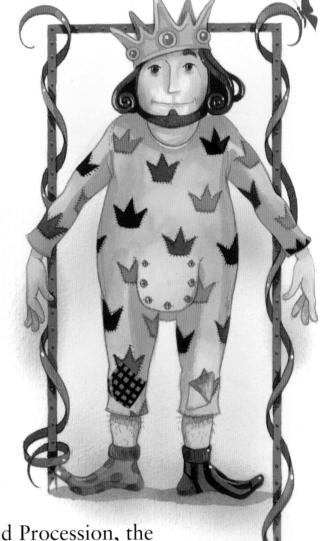

On the morning of the Grand Procession, the Emperor stood in his underwear while the weavers helped him on with his clothes. He agreed with everything they had to say about the cut and the cloth. By the time he had walked up and down a few times, so that the weavers, as they said, could see how well the train draped, he had persuaded himself that he could almost see the costume, and that it was very fine indeed.

So it was that the Emperor walked proudly out at the head of his royal regiment wearing only his second-best pair of royal underwear.

At first, there was a stunned silence from the crowd lining the streets. But everyone had heard that only clever people could see the clothes, so first one and then another spectator cried out, "Wonderful! Superb!" as the Emperor passed. Before long, almost everyone was applauding and cheering. The Emperor felt on top of the world.

Now, it sometimes happens when everyone is making a lot of noise that there is suddenly a brief silence, and one of these silences happened just as the Emperor reached the Great Square. In that moment of quiet, the voice of a little boy could be heard clearly all around the square. "But Mother," he cried, "the Emperor isn't wearing any clothes!"

In that dreadful moment, the whole crowd realized that it was true, and they had been as silly as the Emperor. One by one, the people began to laugh. The Emperor struggled to remain dignified for a second. Then, scooping his imaginary train over one arm, he ran in a most unroyal way back to the palace.

It is said that the Emperor never was quite so vain about clothes after that, and perhaps he had the wicked weavers to thank for it. But those two rascals had become as invisible as the Emperor's famous costume and were never seen again.

THE PRINCESS AND THE PEA

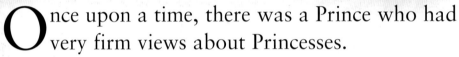

Once upon a time, there was a Prince who had very firm views about Princesses.

"Many of them are simply not Princesses," he said airily.

"My dear, whatever do you mean?" asked his mother the Queen. "Of course they are real Princesses. What about that perfectly charming girl we met last week?"

"She spoke unkindly to her maid," said the Prince.

"Yes, yes, my boy, but Princess Pearl from Argentia was sweetness itself, surely," urged the King.

"She was *silly*," said the Prince.

"But Princess Petronella, so delightful, so accomplished, so refreshing," cried the King and Queen together.

"She was not a *real* Princess at all," said the Prince. "She talked all the time and never listened to a word anyone else said. Real Princesses are ... well, they're ... that is, they seem ... oh, I don't know!"

"I do wish he could meet someone and settle down," sighed the King, as the Prince rushed from the room. "But how are we ever to be sure that a girl is a real Princess? Nowadays, it's so difficult to be sure. I believe I married the last real Princess myself."

"My dear," said the Queen with a smile, "if the right girl comes along, I know exactly how to make sure that she is what she seems. Just leave it to me."

That year, the Prince rode far and wide. He visited many countries and met many pretty Princesses, but he found fault with every one of them. At last, as winter approached, he returned home, more lonely than ever before.

But one night, as the King and Queen and the Prince sat in front of a roaring fire, there came a deafening knocking at the door of the castle.

"Some poor fellow is out in the storm," said the King. "We must let him in to warm himself."

"But, my dear," his wife protested, "we don't know who it is."

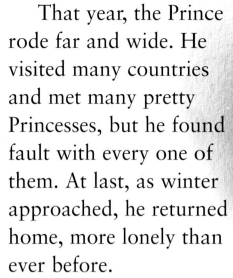

But the King was already striding toward the door. The wind blew so hard that he could hardly stand upright as he pulled it open.

Outside in the courtyard stood a rain-drenched figure. The King had to peer more closely to see that it was not a man at all, but a young girl, shivering in a thin cloak.

"My dear child," cried the King. "Come in at once! Whatever can you be doing out and about on a night like this?"

"My carriage overturned, and I was forced to go in search of shelter," replied the girl, as she came inside. "And you would be surprised how few people are prepared to help a real Princess when she knocks on their door."

The King and Queen exchanged a glance. "Did you say a *real* Princess?" asked the King.

"Of course," his visitor replied. "My father is a King, after all."

"Well, that is interesting," said the King. "I wonder, have you met my son, the Prince?"

The Prince hurried forward at once to kiss the Princess's dainty hand. In fact, he had been unable to take his eyes off the visitor since she first began to drip onto the royal carpet!

"I will have a room prepared for you at once," said the Queen, hurrying from the room.

An hour later, the Princess was tucked up in her room, and the Prince wandered off to walk up and down the corridors, lost in a warm glow of imagining.

● The King could not wait to consult his wife.

● "Well?" he whispered. "What do you think? The boy seems rather taken with her, but is she the real thing?"

● "We'll soon know about that," said the Queen. "I have put twenty mattresses on her bed. Below the bottom mattress I have placed a dried pea. Now we shall see what we shall see."

● "Ah," said the King, "the old pea trick, eh?" Though in truth he had not the faintest idea what the Queen was talking about.

Next morning, the members of the royal family were ~ for different reasons ~ not at all able to concentrate on their breakfast. Things did not improve when their visitor entered the room.

As the Prince hurried to find the pretty girl a chair, the Queen leaned forward eagerly.

"My dear," she said, "I do hope you had a quiet and restful night."

"I'm afraid not," replied the girl, "although you made me so welcome and comfortable. Yet I tossed and turned all night long, and this morning I am black and blue. It's as though there was a boulder under my mattresses."

At that the Queen beamed at her son. "Here," she said, "is a real Princess, my boy. Only a girl with truly royal blood would have skin so tender that she could feel a tiny pea through twenty mattresses. You have my blessing."

"And mine," cried the King, jumping up to clap his son on the shoulder.

Luckily, it was soon discovered that the Princess had fallen as much in love with the Prince as he had with her. They were married soon after, amid great rejoicing.

Well, that was many years ago now, but the royal museum still contains a rather wrinkled green exhibit. You can see it for yourself, if you care to visit.

THE SNOW QUEEN

Our story begins with a mirror owned by a wicked sorcerer. To his delight, the mirror made everything look ugly and twisted, no matter how beautiful it really was. When people looked in the mirror, they said to themselves, "How stupid I've been. Everything is horrid, and it's not worth trying to be good or kind." One day, the mirror broke, and thousands of tiny pieces went flying across the world. Some were so small that people didn't feel it when a tiny fragment flew into their eyes. They only noticed that everything suddenly looked spoiled and dirty. Worse still were the tiny sharp slivers that flew into people's hearts. They turned them to ice, so that they could not feel love and happiness anymore.

Meanwhile, a little girl and boy who lived opposite each other were playing happily high above the busy street. Their houses were built so that each floor was wider than the one below, so the tops of the houses almost touched. There were window boxes on the top floor, in which flowers and roses had been planted. In the summer, the little girl, who was called Gerda, and the little boy, who was called Kay, played together in their tiny garden, while the roses twined above them.

In the winter, when the windows were shut, they had to run down all the stairs in the houses to meet indoors. They watched the snowflakes swirling through the window like a flock of white bees.

"There is a Queen of the Snow just as there is a Queen Bee," said Kay's Grandmother. "She is the biggest snowflake, whirling in the storm."

That evening, when Kay was getting ready for bed, he peered through the window and saw one large snowflake landing on the window box. Before his eyes, it seemed to grow into a beautiful woman, dressed all in white. Her eyes shone like stars, and she seemed to shimmer like ice. Kay knew that she was the Snow Queen. He thought she was the loveliest person he had ever seen. But her eyes were cold, and when she beckoned to the little boy, he turned away from the window and snuggled down in his warm bed. For a second, it seemed as if the shadow of a big black bird flew across the window.

The next day, when Kay and Gerda were playing outside, Kay suddenly gave a little cry.

"Oh," he said, "I just felt a sharp pain in my heart, as if something stabbed me, and it felt as though something flew into my eye, too. But I feel better now."

Tiny pieces of the sorcerer's mirror were now lodged in Kay's eye and heart, which was turned to ice. Seeing Gerda's worried little face, Kay spoke coldly.

"What's the matter with you, Gerda? You don't look at all pretty like that. I'm going off to play with the other boys in the square."

"But we were going to look at my new picture book," said Gerda.

"That's just for babies," shouted Kay, already halfway down the street with his little sled. It was not the real Kay talking, but the ice in his heart.

In the square, there was thick snow. As Kay sat on his toy sled, a magnificent full-sized sleigh swept into the square. It was pulled by white horses and moving like an icy wind. In a flash, Kay stretched out his hands and grabbed hold of the sleigh, so that he was pulled along behind it. Faster and faster they went, out of the city and into the whirling, white countryside.

As the sleigh flew over the fields, the snow swirled thicker around Kay. He began to be rather frightened.

At last the strange sleigh stopped, and the white figure driving it stood up. Kay could see that it was the Snow Queen, dressed in a cloak of white fur.

"Are you cold, little Kay?" she asked. "Come here under my cloak." Kay looked up at the Snow Queen and thought she was more beautiful than ever. He was no longer afraid but flew on with her in the moonlight, gazing at the twinkling stars above the sparkling snow.

Back in the city, little Gerda learned that Kay had disappeared. All through the winter she felt lost and alone, wondering where her friend had gone. Everyone said that he must be dead, but Gerda could not believe that. As soon as spring arrived, she set off to find Kay in her new red shoes.

Gerda soon reached the countryside. Before long, she saw a large orchard, full of cherry trees. There was a little house there too, with red and blue windows. Out of the house came an old woman. She wore a straw hat, covered with beautiful flowers.

Gerda was glad to see a friendly face. Soon she had told the old woman all about Kay.

"I haven't seen him," said the old woman, "but he is sure to come along sooner or later. You can stay here and wait."

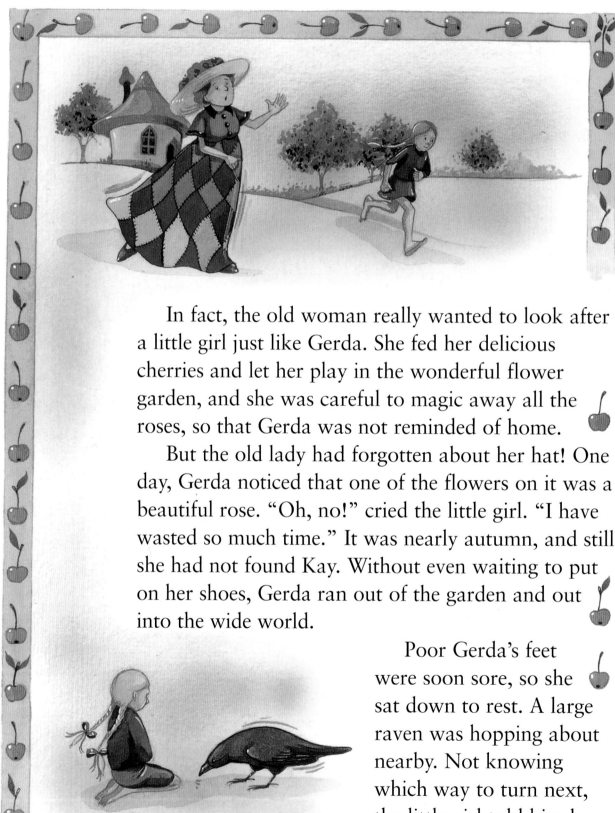

In fact, the old woman really wanted to look after a little girl just like Gerda. She fed her delicious cherries and let her play in the wonderful flower garden, and she was careful to magic away all the roses, so that Gerda was not reminded of home.

But the old lady had forgotten about her hat! One day, Gerda noticed that one of the flowers on it was a beautiful rose. "Oh, no!" cried the little girl. "I have wasted so much time." It was nearly autumn, and still she had not found Kay. Without even waiting to put on her shoes, Gerda ran out of the garden and out into the wide world.

Poor Gerda's feet were soon sore, so she sat down to rest. A large raven was hopping about nearby. Not knowing which way to turn next, the little girl told him her story and asked his advice.

"I may have seen Kay," said the raven, "but he has forgotten all about you. He thinks only of the Princess."

"Is he living with a Princess?" asked Gerda. ✖ Then the raven told her about a Princess who was very clever. When she had read all the books in the castle and was bored, she decided to look for a husband. But he must on no account be a stupid man. ✖ The Princess advertised for a husband, and before long, the grand staircase of the castle was packed with young men lining up to see her. Unfortunately, when they came into her presence, all of them were too amazed by her pearl throne and the rich decorations to say a word, so the Princess sent them away.

"But what about Kay?" asked Gerda impatiently.

Then the raven told how a boy who was not afraid of anyone came along and delighted the Princess by talking with her about all the things that interested her.

"Oh, that must be Kay. He is always so clever," said Gerda. "I must get into that castle and see him!"

"I will see what I can do," cawed the raven, and he flew away.

At evening, the raven came back. "My sweetheart, who lives in the castle, will let you in through a little back door," he said. "Come quickly!"

So Gerda hurried to the castle, where another raven was waiting. She crept up the back stairs. As she did so, she felt that she almost saw swift shadows of swishing skirts and horses and soldiers flitting past. The raven explained that these were the dreams of the ladies and gentlemen sleeping inside.

At last Gerda reached the Princess's room. There, sleeping soundly, was a young man. The little girl crept closer and pulled away the cover. It wasn't Kay!

Gerda was so disappointed that she burst into tears, waking the Prince and Princess. At first she thought they would be angry, but they felt sorry for the little girl and did what they could to help her. They gave her some new boots and a golden carriage, with footmen to take her on her way.

But Gerda's adventures were not over. As she passed in her carriage through a dark forest, some robbers jumped out, pulling her from her seat. They could see that the carriage was worth a fortune. Those robbers might well have killed Gerda at once, if it hadn't been for a little robber girl, who decided to take Gerda back to the robbers' broken-down castle. There she showed Gerda her pet reindeer, but she did not seem to treat him very well.

That night Gerda found it difficult to sleep. High above her head in the rafters, some wood pigeons began to coo. "We have seen little Kay riding through the sky in the Snow Queen's sleigh," they said softly. "She was probably going to Lapland, for the snow and ice never melt there."

"That's true," said the reindeer quietly. "The Snow Queen has her summer palace near the North Pole. I know, for I was born near there."

The next morning, the little robber girl spoke to Gerda. "I heard everything last night," she said. "I will let the reindeer go if he will promise to carry you to Lapland to find Kay."

The reindeer jumped for joy, and Gerda was so happy that she cried. She climbed on the reindeer's back. Night and day they flew through the forest and mountains, until the reindeer pointed out the beautiful northern lights and told Gerda that they had arrived in Lapland.

There was a poor cottage nearby. Shivering with cold, Gerda told her story to the woman who lived there.

"You poor child," said the woman. "I'm afraid you have many miles to go yet. The Snow Queen's palace is in Finland. I will write you a note to a Finnish woman I know. She will help you when you get there."

Once again, Gerda and the reindeer flew over the snowy landscape, until they reached the Finnish woman's home. There was a huge fire inside, so that the inside of the hut was as hot as the outside was cold. The Finnish woman wore hardly any clothes because of the heat, and she immediately helped Gerda off with her coat and boots.

When she had read the note from her friend in Lapland, the Finnish woman looked at Gerda and the reindeer.

"Can't you give Gerda some special magic, so that she can defeat the Snow Queen?" asked the reindeer.

"Gerda doesn't need any special magic," said the Finnish woman. "Her good heart is all the magic she needs. Kay *is* with the Snow Queen. He is happy there because he has a heart of ice and a fragment of the sorcerer's mirror in his eye. Take Gerda out to the edge of the Snow Queen's garden and put her down by a bush with red berries."

The reindeer did as the Finnish woman suggested, although he was sorry to leave Gerda all alone in the cold snow with her bare feet.

Almost at once, Gerda was surrounded by whirling snowflakes. Some seemed ugly and twisted. They moved threateningly toward her, like soldiers. But other snowflakes, like white angels, led her on.

And so it was that Gerda came at last to the Snow Queen's palace, with its walls of snow and doors and windows of bitter winds. Only Gerda's goodness kept her warm as she walked into a huge ice chamber.

There in the middle was little Kay, moving blocks of ice around as if he was trying to solve the most important puzzle in the world.

"Oh, Kay!" cried Gerda, running toward him. Kay stood stiff and cold. He was so pale that he looked almost blue, and he did not greet the little girl who had come so far to find him.

But as Gerda threw her arms around Kay, her warm tears of joy dripped onto his face and heart, melting the ice and washing away the slivers of mirror. The warmth gradually returned to his cheeks, and he too cried at the sight of his very best friend.

Outside, the reindeer was waiting. The children began their long journey home. As they went, the snow melted and the grass and flowers smelled sweet beneath their feet. At last they saw their own city stretching out before them. Holding hands, they ran through the streets they knew so well.

It was as though nothing had changed. Grandmother still sat by the window, and the flowers and roses bloomed in the window boxes high above the street. There Gerda and Kay sat as they had sat before. They were older and wiser, but in their hearts they were children still, and all around them was warmth and light and summer.

THE EMPEROR AND THE NIGHTINGALE

Long ago, the great empire of China had a mighty Emperor. His magnificent palace was built of fragile porcelain and stood in the most beautiful garden the world has ever seen. Not only were the flowers exquisite, but the gardeners had hung tiny silver bells among them, so that they tinkled little tunes among the blooms.

At the end of the gardens was a wonderful forest, and beyond the forest the deep blue sea stretched far away. It was here, at the edge of the water, that a nightingale had made its home. Sitting in the branches of a stately tree, the nightingale each evening opened her heart and sang so beautifully that even the hard-working fishermen stopped their work to hear her liquid notes.

Many strangers came to the imperial palace to gasp at the porcelain and the treasures inside. Of course, they were equally amazed by the intricate gardens and the trees beyond. But every visitor who heard the song of the nightingale could not help exclaiming, "Everything here is wonderful beyond belief, but nothing compares to the song of this magical bird."

When they returned to their own countries, some of the visitors wrote books describing the extraordinary things they had seen, and all of them ended by praising the nightingale's song above everything else.

Now the Emperor was very fond of reading books about his country, and he was especially fond of reading about his amazing palace and its grounds. He felt proud to be the owner of such magnificence. You can imagine his surprise when he first read an account that rated the nightingale's song more highly than all his costly possessions.

"Why have I never heard the song of this bird, although she lives within my grounds?" he asked his courtiers. "Bring her to me tonight, for I must hear her sing."

The courtiers had never heard of the nightingale. They ran all over the palace, searching for someone who had heard of her, but with no success.

"Perhaps the story in your book has been invented by the author, Your Imperial Highness," suggested the courtiers.

"Nonsense," said the Emperor. "You must all search harder."

The courtiers were almost at their wits' ends when they found a young maid in the Emperor's enormous kitchens.

"I have heard the nightingale sing many times, when I go down to the shore to visit my mother," she said. "It is a truly wonderful sound."

The courtiers insisted that the kitchen maid lead them to the nightingale's tree, but they themselves had no idea what her song would be like. As they walked through the forest beyond the gardens, they heard a deep, booming sound.

"What a beautiful song," they cried. "We have found the nightingale."

"No, no," said the kitchen maid. "That is a cow calling to its calf."

Next the courtiers heard a bubbling, chirping sound.

"There, that is the nightingale," they declared. "How beautiful!"

"No," replied the kitchen maid, looking at them in amazement. "That is a frog, calling across a pond."

Just then the nightingale began to sing. A ribbon of beautiful sound shimmered in the air. The kitchen maid pointed to a little brown bird on a branch.

"That is the nightingale," she said.

The courtiers were amazed that such a drab bird could make such a beautiful sound, but they invited her to the palace that evening, as the Emperor had commanded. The nightingale was astonished that she should be summoned in such a way, but she went along willingly to sing to the owner of the palace and the gardens and the forest and the sea.

The entire court gathered with the Emperor to hear the nightingale sing that evening. A special golden stand had been made for her to perch on.

As the nightingale's first notes trembled in the air, tears rolled down the Emperor's cheeks. He had never heard anything so beautiful. Everyone else in the room was equally moved. The little bird was a great success.

After that, the nightingale had to live at the palace. She had her own golden cage and twelve servants. Twice a day, she was allowed to fly around a little, but one of the servants kept hold of a silken thread attached to her leg, so she was never allowed to fly free.

One day, a present arrived for the Emperor. It was a mechanical bird, made of gold and silver and precious jewels. When it was wound up with a golden key, the bird sang one of the nightingale's songs, moving its shining tail. It was a gift from the Emperor of Japan.

The mechanical bird sang very well, and what is more, it always sang exactly the same song, over and over again. The real nightingale sang as her heart told her, sometimes happily, sometimes sadly, sometimes loudly, sometimes softly.

"This mechanical bird will never disappoint you, Your Imperial Highness," said the Court Musician. "And she is much more beautiful than the real nightingale."

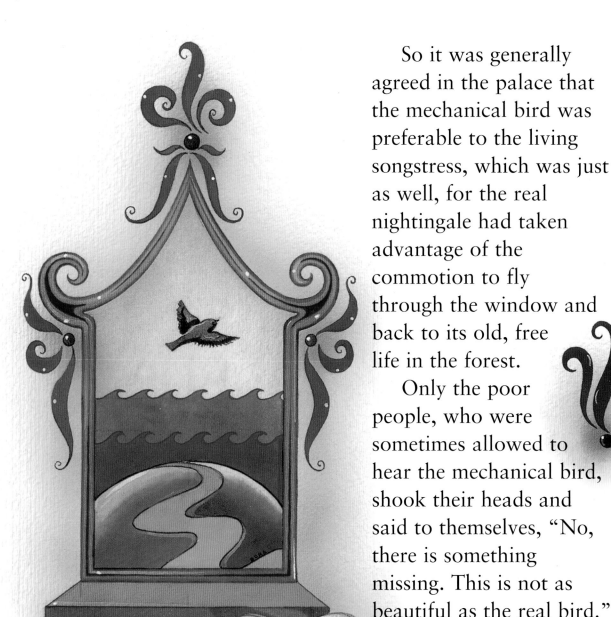

So it was generally agreed in the palace that the mechanical bird was preferable to the living songstress, which was just as well, for the real nightingale had taken advantage of the commotion to fly through the window and back to its old, free life in the forest.

Only the poor people, who were sometimes allowed to hear the mechanical bird, shook their heads and said to themselves, "No, there is something missing. This is not as beautiful as the real bird."

A year passed. The mechanical nightingale sat on a silken cushion on the Emperor's left side, which was a position of great privilege. But one day when the bird was wound up with the golden key as usual, it merely said, "Krrrrr. Krrrrr." The bird had sung so often that its mechanism was worn out.

Luckily, the Court Watchmaker was able to repair the bird, but he warned that in future she must only sing once a year.

Several years passed, and the people of China were shocked to learn that their Emperor was dangerously ill. He lay, pale and cold, on his magnificent bed. The courtiers were so sure that he was about to die that they began to pay court to the man who would be the next Emperor.

In the middle of the night, as the moonlight streamed through his open window, the Emperor was visited by fears and phantoms. "Sing!" he begged the mechanical nightingale at his side, hoping to drown out his dark thoughts. But there was no one to wind up the wonderful bird, so it remained silent.

Suddenly, through the open window, the Emperor heard a wonderful sound. It was the real nightingale, perched on a branch outside and singing her heart out. As she sang, the Emperor's fevered mind was soothed, and his illness left him.

"Thank you, little bird," he gasped. "I don't deserve your help after the way I treated you. But now you must remain in my palace and sing to me every day."

"No, My Lord," said the nightingale. "I cannot live in a palace, but I will come of my own free will and sing outside your window as often as I can. And I will do something more for you. I will tell you what the poorest people in your land are thinking and feeling ~ something that you cannot know, surrounded as you are by courtiers eager to impress you. But you must promise never to tell anyone what I am doing."

The Emperor promised gladly and fell into a deep, refreshing sleep. When the servants came at last to look at their dead Emperor, they found him alive and smiling, ready to take up the reins of power again.

The Emperor ruled for many more years, more wisely and well than ever before, but he kept the nightingale's secret to the end of his days.

THE UGLY DUCKLING

One sunny summer day, when the wildflowers were nodding in the heat, a mother duck sat on her nest. She had found a shady spot in some weeds at the edge of the pond.

It seemed to the duck that she had been sitting on her eggs for a very long time. Then, one morning, she heard a tiny sound from one of the eggs. Peep! Peep! A little duckling scuttled out from under her feathers.

All at once, there were little sounds from more of the eggs. Before long, twelve fluffy little ducklings were cuddling up to their mother.

"It's lovely to see you, my dears," she quacked. "The wait has been so long." But one of the eggs ~ the largest of all ~ had not yet hatched. "How annoying," said the mother duck, and she settled down to wait a little longer.

Sure enough, a day or two later, there was a tap-tapping from the egg. First a little beak appeared. Then a little head peeked out. At last a funny little bird stood in the nest.

Well! The mother duck could hardly bear to look at the youngster. He really was the ugliest bird she had ever seen. He didn't look like a duckling at all.

"I'll push him into the water," said the mother duck. "If he cannot swim, I'll know he is a turkey or some other kind of bird."

But when she nudged the untidy bird out into the pond, he swam off quite happily. In fact, he swam so well that the duck felt quite proud of her ugly duckling.

"Come along, my dears," she cried to her children, "and I will introduce you to the other animals in the barnyard. Just watch out for the cat!"

In the barnyard, the other ducks and the hens quacked and clucked in approval as the mother duck led her twelve little ducklings past. But when they saw the last duckling, they shook their heads and hissed and squawked.

"What a horrible bird!" they cried.

"He will grow into his feathers," replied the mother duck. "And I must tell you that he swims better than all my ducklings." She shepherded her brood back to the pond.

As the ducklings grew, they loved to swim and dive in the pond. Then they would waddle in the barnyard, shaking their feathers. But the ugly duckling soon dreaded the barnyard birds. They pecked at him and called him names. Every day it grew worse.

At last a morning came when the little duckling could bear it no longer. He ran and fluttered as fast as his legs could carry him away from the barnyard.

As night fell, he came, tired and hungry, to a wild marsh, where little frogs jumped and croaked in the moonlight. In the morning, the wild ducks who lived there found a stranger among them.

"We've never seen a duck as ugly as you!" they laughed. "But you can live here if you like, as long as you don't get in our way."

The little duckling was still lonely, but at least no one bullied him. Then one morning, as he swam by the bank, he suddenly saw a dog running through the reeds. All around the marsh, hunters and their dogs were gathering.

The little duckling hid in the reeds all day, trembling with fright as shots whistled over his bowed head.

That night, he once again fled as fast as he could from his unsafe home.

The weather was growing colder, and the wind was ruffling his feathers, when he came to a tumbledown cottage and crept inside to escape the coming storm.

An old woman lived in the cottage with her cat and her hen. She let the duckling stay, but the cat and hen were not very friendly.

"Can you lay eggs?" they asked. "Or purr, or catch mice?"

"No," whispered the duckling.

"Then you are no use at all," said the cat and hen.

At last, the duckling could bear the unkindness no longer. He wandered out into the world once more.

When the duckling came to a lake, he realized how much he had missed swimming. It was lovely to glide across the water in the moonlight. But winter was coming, and the nights grew colder.

One frosty day, at sunset, a flock of beautiful white birds flew over the lake. The duckling did not know that they were swans, but he longed to see them again. He felt that he had never seen anything so lovely.

The days grew colder and colder. One morning, the poor duckling woke to find that he had become trapped in the frozen water. Luckily, a passing farmer freed him and carried him home to his family.

But the youngster was frightened by the children's attempts to play with him. As he clumsily flapped his wings, he knocked over dishes and made a terrible mess. The farmer's wife chased him from the house.

Once again, the young bird was on his own. He struggled through the rest of the winter.

But gradually, the days became lighter. The grass began to grow, and spring flowers appeared. The bird found that his wings were stronger, and he could fly swiftly over the water. One afternoon, he caught sight of the beautiful white birds he loved so much far below.

"I must talk to them, just once," thought the young bird, "even if they attack me because I am so ugly."

As he landed, the swans rushed toward him, beating their wings. The bird bowed his head, waiting for their attack. As he did so, he saw his reflection. He wasn't an ugly duckling at all! Through the winter months he had grown up ... into a beautiful white swan! The other swans had come to welcome him.

No bird was ever so happy, as he swam with his new friends. Later, two children came to feed the swans.

"Oh look," they cried, "there's a new one! And he's the most beautiful swan of all!"

THE SHADOW

Once there was a writer who went from a cold country to a hot one. He could not go out in the daytime, for it was just too hot. In the evening, when it was cooler, the streets were filled with people.

Opposite the man's home was a house that seemed to be empty, yet lovely music came from it. As he sat on his balcony one night, with the lighted room behind, the man saw that his shadow seemed to be sitting on the opposite balcony.

"If only you could go inside for me and see who is there," said the man. And, you know, when he got up and went inside, the shadow did look as though it went into the house opposite.

The next morning, the man was astonished to find that he had no shadow at all! At first he was worried about this, but after a few days he noticed that a new shadow was beginning to grow, and by the time he returned to his home in the cold country, the shadow was as long as it ever was.

Several years passed, and one evening, when the man was writing in his room, there was a knock at the door. Standing outside was a very thin man, who gave our hero goose pimples all over.

"I suppose you don't recognize me," said the visitor, "now that I have become so human. I am your old shadow. I have become rich and wise since I left you, but I wanted to see you again one more time."

"But what happened to you?" asked the man in astonishment.

Then the Shadow described how he had entered the house opposite and found that a goddess named Poetry lived there.

"Even standing in the hallway, I found that it was as though I saw everything in the world and understood everything too," said the Shadow. "A great desire came upon me to be a man, but I had no clothes or money. The next day ~ don't laugh! ~ I hid under the baker woman's skirts and didn't come out until nighttime. Then I ran here and there, telling people truths about themselves that even they did not know. And they were so grateful and so afraid that their friends would find out that they gave me rich presents and the fine clothes you see me in today."

Then the Shadow politely took his leave.

A year passed, and the Shadow called on his old master again.

"Things are going even better for me," he said. "Look, I have grown quite plump. How are things with you?"

"I still write my books about goodness and beauty and truth," said the man, "but no one wants to read them."

"Listen," said the Shadow. "I feel like taking a trip and I would like a companion. Will you come with me ~ as my shadow?"

"That's crazy," said the man. "Of course not."

But the next year, the man became tired and ill.
"You look like a shadow!" said his friends.

When the Shadow called again, the man agreed
that a warmer climate would be good for his health.
So he set off with the Shadow, and stayed at his side all
the time, as a good shadow should.

At last the Shadow and *his* shadow reached a spa,
where people go to get better from illnesses. Also
staying there was a Princess, who saw very clearly.

"I know why you are here," she said to the
Shadow. "You cannot cast a real shadow!"

"That's nonsense," cried the Shadow. "Look, there
he is. I treat him so well, giving him clothes and food,
that he has become almost human."

So the Princess talked to the shadow-man, and
found him very intelligent.

Then the Princess thought, "I will marry this man
who is so extraordinary that even his shadow is wise."
And she took the Shadow to her own country.

As the wedding preparations were made, the Shadow said to the man, "Listen, I will give you money and a state coach if only you will always stay with me and never tell a soul that I was once your shadow."

"Never!" cried the man. "You are mad!"

Then the Shadow ran quickly to the girl, looking shocked and pale.

"Oh, a dreadful thing has happened," he told her. "My shadow has gone crazy and thinks he is human. I have had to have him locked away!"

"It might be better," said the Princess, "if he never appeared again."

So that night, when the wedding took place, the Shadow's shadow was not there, and he has never been seen since.

THE TINDERBOX

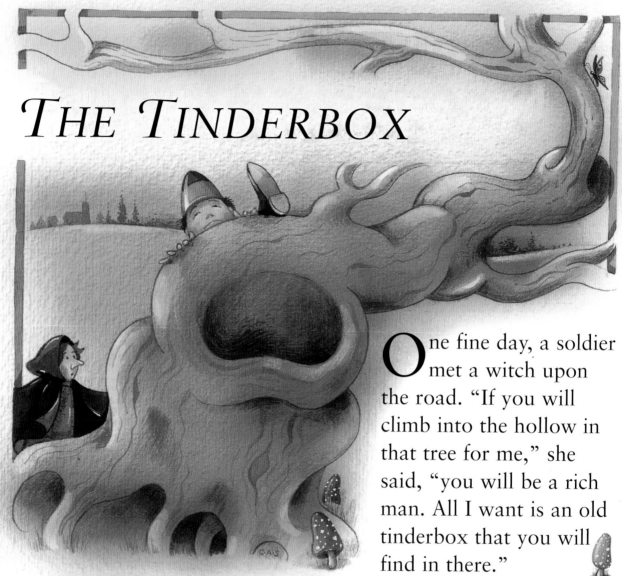

One fine day, a soldier met a witch upon the road. "If you will climb into the hollow in that tree for me," she said, "you will be a rich man. All I want is an old tinderbox that you will find in there."

The soldier had always wanted to be rich, so he agreed. Inside the tree, as the witch had told him, were three rooms. In each room was a chest of money, guarded by a fierce dog. The first had eyes as round as saucers. The second had eyes as big as mill wheels. The third had huge eyes, like round towers. But the witch had also told the soldier how to deal with the dogs, so he quickly filled his pockets and hat with money. Then, picking up the old tinderbox, he climbed out of the tree.

The soldier wondered why the witch wanted the tinderbox so badly, but she refused to tell him.

"You can cut off my head before I'll say a word," she said. So the soldier did!

After that, the soldier lived a wonderful life, with rich food and wine, handsome clothes and fine friends. But in a surprisingly short time, all his money was spent. Now he lived in an attic room, with only the stub of a candle for light.

One evening, the soldier felt in his pocket and found the old tinderbox. He thought he would use it to light his last candle. But as he struck a spark from the flint, the dog with eyes as round as saucers appeared before him. Two strikes, and the dog with eyes as big as mill wheels appeared. With three strikes, the soldier could summon the dog with huge eyes, like round towers. And the dogs were ready to do whatever the soldier asked, bringing him money, jewels, and other fine things.

Soon the soldier was as rich and happy as he had been before. One day, he heard that the King and Queen of the country had a beautiful daughter, but that she was hardly ever seen. Feeling curious, he sent the first dog to fetch her.

As soon as he saw the Princess, the soldier wanted more than anything to marry her. He kissed her and reluctantly sent her back to the palace.

The next morning, the Princess told the King and Queen that she had had a curious dream of being kissed by a soldier. At once, the royal pair decided to keep a close watch on their daughter.

Each night, the soldier could not help sending one of his dogs to fetch the Princess. It was not long before the King and Queen tracked him down. He was quickly thrown into prison and sentenced to death.

"If only I had my tinderbox with me," said the soldier. At last, he managed to give a message to a little boy outside his window, who ran off at once to fetch the tinderbox.

With the tinderbox in his hand once more, the soldier knew that nothing could hurt him. He summoned the three dogs, who quickly overpowered the guards and chased away the King and Queen, who had come to watch the execution.

The people were happy to offer the throne to the Princess, and she was happy to accept it ~ and the hand of the handsome soldier whose face she had seen in her dreams. So the soldier lived happily ever after, and the most pampered guests in the royal palace were ... his dogs, of course!

THE FIR TREE

Once upon a time, a little fir tree grew in a forest. All around him were beautiful trees. The sunlight flecked his branches with gold, and the wind sighed around him. But the little fir tree was not happy. He longed to be bigger.

Time passed. Each year, the tree grew taller and his branches spread.

"Perhaps I will soon be cut down," he said, "as the biggest trees are each year. Then I will travel over the sea. How wonderful that will be!"

The storks had told the little tree that the largest trees were made into the masts of ships. Each year at Christmas time, some smaller trees were cut down, too.

"They are taken into people's homes," said the sparrows, "and decorated with toys and jewels."

That sounded even better to the little fir tree, although the sparrows did not seem to know what happened to the trees after Christmas.

All this time, the fir tree could think of nothing but growing bigger. He was very beautiful, but he cared nothing for his lovely home and the blue sky above. All he wanted was to be grown up and gone.

And, of course, the little tree did grow. The very next Christmas, he was one of the first to be cut down.

Down in the town, the fir tree was chosen by a very grand family and carried back to their magnificent home. How proud he felt, covered with candles, ornaments, and presents. But he was too busy wondering what would happen next to feel really happy.

That night, the children danced around the tree and opened their presents. It was such a pretty sight!

Next morning, some servants removed the rest of the decorations and put the tree away in a storeroom, with lots of old boxes and junk. Only the golden star on his highest branch remained.

The tree was lonely in the storeroom, until some little mice came to talk to him. They wanted to hear about his life in the open forest, and all that he had seen and done in the great house.

"How happy you must have been!" they cried.

"I suppose I was," said the fir tree. "But I did not feel happy then."

Some months later, when the fir tree was yellow and dry, he was taken out into the yard.

"Look at that ugly old tree!" cried the children, who were playing outside. They stamped on his brittle branches and broke them.

Then the tree realized how happy he had been in the storeroom, where no one had troubled him. But he had not felt happy at the time.

Before long, a servant came. He chopped up the tree for firewood. Piece by piece, the poor tree was burned on the kitchen stove.

"How happy I was in the yard," he sighed, giving off little crackles and pops as he was thrown into the flames.

At last all the tree was gone. Poor tree! In all his wonderful life, he had always been wishing for something else, and never felt truly happy. You won't be like him, will you?

THE BRAVE TIN SOLDIER

Once there was a box of twenty-five tin soldiers. They all looked exactly the same, with smart red and blue uniforms and rifles on their shoulders, except that the last one had only one leg, for the toymaker had run out of tin when he was made.

But the last tin soldier could stand up as straight as his brothers, and he was just as brave. At night, when their little owner had gone to bed, all the toys jumped up and played by themselves.

The last tin soldier looked all around, and he noticed a fine toy castle, with a lady at the door. He saw that she was very pretty, wearing a beautiful dress. And she only had one leg, too!

"She would make a fine wife for me," said the tin soldier, and he climbed up on a box so that he could see her more clearly.

In fact, the pretty lady was a dancer, standing on one leg. Her other leg was tucked under her skirts. The tin soldier did not know this, and he did not know that he was sitting on a jack-in-the-box! At midnight, the box burst open, and the soldier went flying over to the windowsill.

Next morning, when the windows were opened, the little soldier fell out! Down, down, he went, until he landed upside down with his rifle sticking into the pavement. Although his owner came down at once to look for him, he went sadly back indoors when it started to rain.

The rain was heavy, but it ended at last, and two boys coming down the street *did* see where the toy soldier had fallen.

"Let's make a paper boat," they said, "and send him off along the running water."

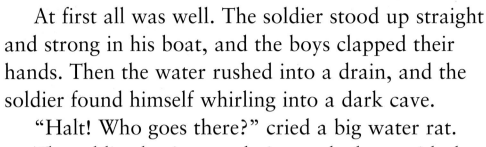

At first all was well. The soldier stood up straight and strong in his boat, and the boys clapped their hands. Then the water rushed into a drain, and the soldier found himself whirling into a dark cave.

"Halt! Who goes there?" cried a big water rat.

The soldier, having no choice, rushed on, with the water rat running behind him.

The noise of the rushing water became louder and louder. To his horror, the tin soldier saw that he was sailing toward a huge waterfall, where the water poured into the canal. Before he could do anything, the boat sank altogether, leaving the soldier floundering.

Just at that moment, a passing fish opened its jaws and ... swallowed the soldier whole!

The tin soldier lay still inside the fish for a long time. Suddenly, he saw a flash of light and heard a cry. "The tin soldier!" The fish had been caught and taken to market. Now the cook who had bought it was cutting it open. And this was not just any cook! In five minutes, the tin soldier found himself back in the nursery with his brothers.

The tin soldier looked longingly at the pretty lady in the castle, for she had never left his heart. And she looked longingly at him.

But the soldier's adventures were not over. A little boy threw him into the fire. Brave to the last, the little man stood and felt himself melting. At that moment, a rush of air sent the pretty lady flying into the fire to join him. The soldier and his lady were together at last.

Next morning, when he raked out the fire, a servant found a tin heart ~ all that was left of the brave soldier and his lady love.

THE WILD SWANS

Once there was a King who had eleven sons and one little daughter, called Eliza. They were beautiful, happy children, although their mother had died many years before.

But one day, the King married a wicked Queen, who did not love the children. She sent Eliza to live with a poor family far from the palace and turned the boys into wild swans.

The years passed, and Eliza grew up to be both lovely and good. When she was fifteen, her father sent for her. As soon as she saw her pretty face, the wicked Queen hated Eliza even more. She stained the girls skin and tangled her hair, so that her father, when he saw her, shuddered and sent her away.

Friendless and alone, the poor girl wandered from the palace deep into the forest, where she bathed in a crystal stream and became beautiful once more. At night, under the trees, Eliza dreamed of her eleven fine brothers, handsome and grown up now.

The next morning, Eliza met an old woman on the path.

"Have you seen eleven fine Princes?" she asked.

"No," replied the woman, "but yesterday I saw eleven fine swans with crowns on their heads swimming along the stream."

Eliza followed the stream to the sea. There she waited, until at sunset eleven swans with golden crowns came flying toward her. Hiding behind a bush, the girl watched as the swans landed. When darkness came, each swan turned into a handsome Prince once more. With a cry, Eliza ran to be reunited with her brothers.

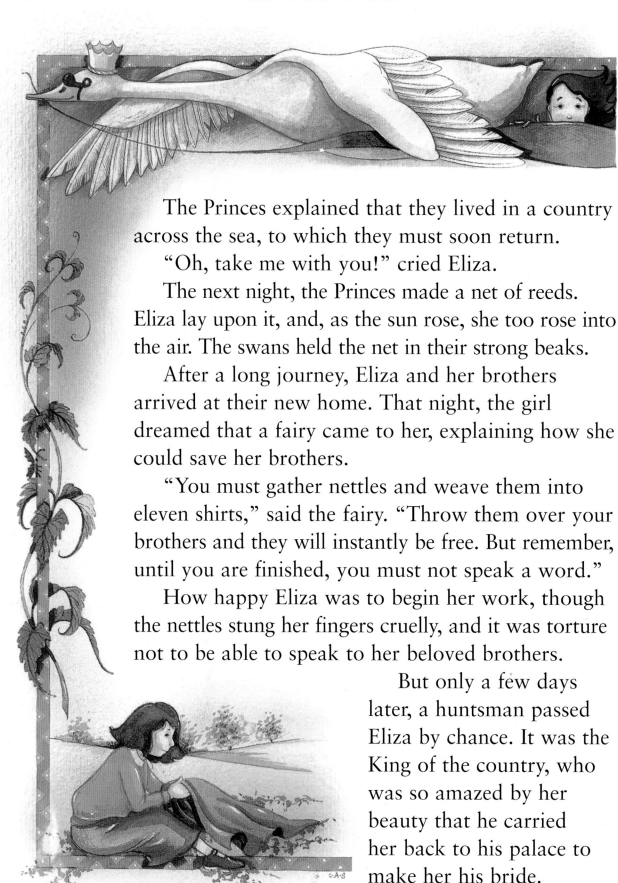

The Princes explained that they lived in a country across the sea, to which they must soon return.

"Oh, take me with you!" cried Eliza.

The next night, the Princes made a net of reeds. Eliza lay upon it, and, as the sun rose, she too rose into the air. The swans held the net in their strong beaks.

After a long journey, Eliza and her brothers arrived at their new home. That night, the girl dreamed that a fairy came to her, explaining how she could save her brothers.

"You must gather nettles and weave them into eleven shirts," said the fairy. "Throw them over your brothers and they will instantly be free. But remember, until you are finished, you must not speak a word."

How happy Eliza was to begin her work, though the nettles stung her fingers cruelly, and it was torture not to be able to speak to her beloved brothers.

But only a few days later, a huntsman passed Eliza by chance. It was the King of the country, who was so amazed by her beauty that he carried her back to his palace to make her his bride.

Eliza tried to escape, but she could not speak to explain her desperate task. Besides, she gradually grew fond of the King, who gave her a room of her own where she could work on the nettle shirts.

The time came when Eliza needed just one more bunch of nettles to finish the last shirts. She crept out of the palace in the dead of night and went to a nearby churchyard, where nettles grew. Unfortunately, the Archbishop, who had always mistrusted her, followed her. He believed that her visit showed she was a witch and he persuaded the King to condemn her to death.

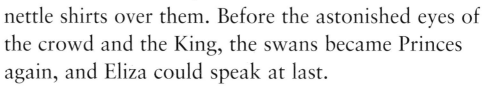

Alone in her prison cell, Eliza worked desperately to finish the shirts in time. At dawn, on the day of her execution, eleven beautiful swans flew down as she was led to the fire. In an instant, she threw the nettle shirts over them. Before the astonished eyes of the crowd and the King, the swans became Princes again, and Eliza could speak at last.

"I am innocent!" she cried.

Weeping with happiness, the King folded her in his arms, while her brothers gathered round. Only the youngest still had a swan's wing instead of an arm, for Eliza had been unable to finish her work before dawn.